W9-COV-719

Max
and
Zoe

The School Concert

by Shelley Swanson Sateren

illustrated by Mary Sullivan

PICTURE WINDOW BOOKS
a capstone imprint

Max and Zoe is published by Picture Window Books
a Capstone Imprint
1710 Roe Crest Drive
North Mankato, Minnesota 56003
www.capstonepub.com

Library of Congress Cataloging-in-Publication Data
Sateren, Shelley Swanson.
 Max and Zoe : the school concert / by Shelley Swanson Sateren ;
illustrated by Mary Sullivan.
    p. cm. -- (Max and Zoe)
 Summary: Max is worried about singing in the school concert, so
his best friend Zoe offers to help him practice.
 ISBN 978-1-4048-7198-4 (library binding)
 1. Singing--Juvenile fiction. 2. Concerts--Juvenile fiction. 3.
Schools--Juvenile fiction. 4. Best friends--Juvenile fiction. [1.
Singing--Fiction. 2. Concerts--Fiction. 3. Schools--Fiction. 4. Best
friends--Fiction. 5. Friendship--Fiction.] I. Sullivan, Mary, 1958-
ill. II. Title. III. Title: School concert. IV. Series: Sateren, Shelley
Swanson. Max and Zoe.

 PZ7.S249155Mds 2012
 813.54--dc23

                           2011051238

Designer: Emily Harris

Printed in the United States of America in Stevens Point, Wisconsin.
062014   008283R

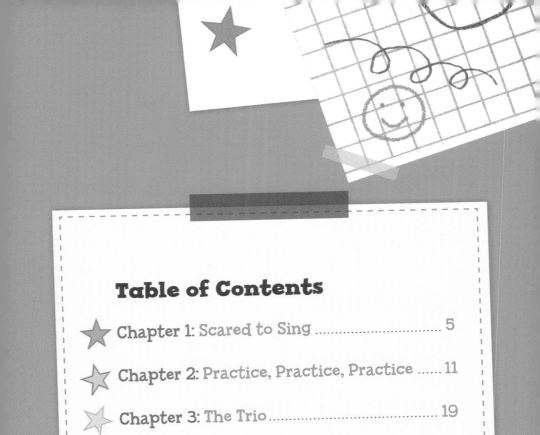

Table of Contents

Chapter 1: Scared to Sing 5

Chapter 2: Practice, Practice, Practice 11

Chapter 3: The Trio 19

Max and Zoe's class

practiced in the music room.

"Next, we will hear 'The

Garden Tune,'" said Mrs.

Lopez, their music teacher.

Henry and Ruby hurried

to the piano.

Max walked slowly.

"Why did I say I'd do this?" thought Max. "I stink at singing."

Henry, Ruby, and Max stood by the piano.

"All right, gardeners," said Mrs. Lopez. "Sing your best. The rest of you hum like honeybees."

Quietly, Henry and Ruby began to sing. But Max couldn't.

His mouth was super dry.

The microphone slid out of

his sweaty fingers.

"I'll totally mess up

tomorrow," he thought.

"Louder, trio!" said

Mrs. Lopez. "Come on,

Max."

Henry and Ruby sang a little louder. Max tried to sing a few words.

"They'll be mad at me tomorrow," he thought. "Everyone will laugh."

After school, Max sat by Zoe on the bus.

"I'm so nervous," he said. "I'm going to throw up."

"No, you're going to practice," said Zoe. "I'll help you."

Chapter 2
Practice, Practice, Practice

Zoe went to Max's

apartment after school.

"Use your comb for a

mic," she said. "Ready? Go."

Max looked at the sheet
music. He began to sing.
Buddy covered his head.

"See?" said Max. "My
singing is terrible."

"Go away, Buddy!" Zoe
said.

Zoe lined up stuffed
animals. "Sing to them," she
said. "But first, breathe deep
five times."

Max did, then started
again.

"Louder," said Zoe.

"Pretend you're excited to

sing on stage!"

Max sang loudly but read

some words wrong.

"Keep going if you mess

up," Zoe said. "People won't

notice."

Max practiced more, but the animals didn't smile. That made Max feel extra nervous.

"I have a better idea," said Zoe. She drew pictures of smiling faces. Then she taped them to Max's wall.

Max sang and sang

to the friendly faces. His

breathing slowed down. He

remembered the words, too.

After Zoe went home,

Max kept practicing.

"Among the bees, we're on our knees, we're digging in the dirt," he sang. "Among the bees, we're on our knees, we're in our gardening shirts!"

By bedtime, Max tossed

the sheet music away. He

was ready.

Chapter 3
The Trio

After lunch the next day,

the concert began.

On stage, the class sang

the opening songs. And then

it was time for the trio.

Max's heart beat fast. He took five deep breaths. Then he picked a very friendly face to look at—his mom's.

Mrs. Lopez began to play the piano. Max opened his mouth to sing.

All of the words came out,

clear and strong! But Ruby

and Henry weren't singing.

Max sang alone for

the entire song. Everyone

cheered. Max bowed.

After the concert,

everyone got milk and

cookies.

"I'm sorry I messed up,"

said Ruby.

"Me too," said Henry.

"It's okay," said Max.

"Everyone gets nervous

sometimes. Here, have my

cookies."

"Really? Thanks,"

they said.

"Wow, Max," Zoe said.

"You sang a solo!"

"I'm so proud of you, Max," said his mom.

"Thanks!" said Max. "I'm proud of me too!"

"And I think that deserves another cookie," said Zoe.

About the Author

Shelley Swanson Sateren is the award-winning author of many children's books. She has worked as a children's book editor and in a children's bookstore. Today, besides writing, Shelley works with elementary-school-aged children in various settings. She lives in St. Paul, Minnesota, with her husband and two sons.

About the Illustrator

Mary Sullivan has been drawing and writing her whole life, which has mostly been spent in Texas. She earned her BFA from the University of Texas in Studio Art, but she considers herself a self-trained illustrator. Mary lives in Cedar Park, a suburb of Austin, Texas.

Glossary

concert (KON-surt) — a show put on by singers or a band

microphone (MYE-kruh-fone) — a stick-like tool that makes sounds louder; also called a mic

nervous (NUR-vuhss) — fearful or timid

practice (PRAK-tiss) — doing something over and over again to get better at it

solo (SOH-loh) — a piece of music that is played or sung by one person

trio (TREE-oh) — a piece of music that is played or sung by three people

Discussion Questions

1. If you had to sing a solo, duet, or trio, which one would you pick? Why?

2. Max learned some tips to feel less nervous. What were they? List some other tips that can help you relax when you feel nervous.

3. Were you surprised by the end of the story? Why or why not?

Writing Prompts

1. Max does a lot of practicing. Write about something that you have practiced.

2. The story introduces part of the song "The Garden Tune." Write more lines to the song.

3. Max is nervous to sing. Write about something that makes you nervous.

Make Your Own Mic

What you need:

- toilet-paper tube
- black construction paper (6 inches long and 4 inches high)
- sheet of aluminum foil (3 feet long)
- craft glue
- scissors

What you do:

1. Glue the black paper onto the tube.

2. Cut off any extra paper. This is the mic's handle.

3. Crunch the foil into a ball. Make the bottom pointy. This is the mic.

4. Put glue inside the top of the tube.

5. Stuff the pointy end of the foil ball into the handle. The top should be a round, silver ball.

6. Let the glue dry.

7. Then grab your mic and sing your favorite songs.

The Fun Doesn't Stop Here!

Discover more at www.capstonekids.com

- Videos & Contests
- Games & Puzzles
- Friends & Favorites
- Authors & Illustrators

Find cool websites and more books like this one at www.facthound.com. Just type in the Book ID **9781404871984** and you're ready to go!

DATE			

8|17- 6